THE LOOKOUT

AND OTHER STORIES

THE **LOOKOUT**

A N D   O T H E R   S T O R I E S

DANIEL GARDINA

KING'S MEN
P R E S S

KING'S MEN
P R E S S

Published by King's Men Press, Los Angeles
www.kingsmenpress.com

"Gone Fishing" first appeared in *Head Wounds,* Spring 2006. "Killing Birds" and "Today's the Day" first appeared in *Book by Authors*, December 2006.

ISBN 978-0-615-63998-7

For Mom, Dad, & Kim.
Thanks for the years of support.

CONTENTS

THE LOOKOUT

AND OTHER STORIES

GONE FISHING

Seamus, already sporting his fishing vest and wading pants, sat alone in the dentist's office. He was dressed and ready for his weekend excursion immediately following his final pit stop where cavities came to be punished. Once at the lake, this preparation would save him the ten extra minutes that would be spent fly-fishing. But first things first, he told himself. The dentist was simply one of those necessary chores. After all, he'd already postponed the appointment twice.

The recessed ceiling speakers chimed with Muzak ditties intended to soothe patrons waiting to have their plaque, tartar, and dignity picked clean. He thought he could make out the tune "Girl From Ipanema." If he were waiting for Miss Ipanema to clean his teeth—that tall and tan and lovely Miss Ipanema, who walked like a samba—maybe he wouldn't mind his rendezvous with the drill. The visit might even be worthwhile so long as he had a pretty face to admire while she burrowed away at his molars.

No, that's just crazy. She could be massaging him and whispering sweet nothings in his ear and still he'd prefer to be elsewhere. As if these trials of mental and physical fortitude weren't enough for one man to endure, the hygienist who experimented on his mouth exhibited the care and precision of a three-year-old given knives to play with. Grizelda always worked on him despite his requests for a different tormentor.

Forget it. He couldn't handle this today.

He stood just as the waiting room door creaked open like a rusted dungeon hatch and Grizelda entered—all two hundred and thirty pounds of her. Her musk distantly resembled baby powder but lacked that Johnson-and-Johnson freshness.

"Next," she said with a smoker's croak.

Seamus froze mid-step. After taking one final look at the exit, he obediently crossed the ragged carpet and marched down the hall. He passed open rooms where fellow inmates gripped their armrests and kicked their feet in tune with the whine of the drill. He grimaced as he entered his own torture cell. The chair reclined, and he squirmed as the headrest cut into the back of his neck, the overhead lamp rattling as he shifted. He leaned over to note the loose bolts barely securing it to the chair. He wondered how long it would take the lamp to fall like a guillotine. At least then he wouldn't have to deal with Grizelda. On the other hand, he wouldn't get to go fishing either.

She unwrapped the sterilized tools and displayed the rudimentary devices on the steel tray under Seamus' nose. He could've sworn he saw her smirk.

"Lean forward," she said.

She rested the paper bib on his chest and swung the chain around his neck.

"Ooo," he said. "Chain's cold."

She raised and dropped her eyebrows as quickly as she probably considered the chain's temperature, let alone how he felt about it. She went ahead and attached the alligator clips to the paper.

"Oh," she said, looking over his chart. "Looks like I saw you last time."

He didn't care to dignify her astuteness with a response. Changing the subject sounded better.

"So... How long have you been a hygienist?"

She coughed three times without covering her mouth. "Twenty years."

He remembered the last time he saw her, when she sliced open his gums with her chisel. He wondered why she hadn't improved during her career. Who knows? Maybe she had. If so, he wondered where her first patients' grave markers were located.

She released the chair's lever without warning. Seamus' body dropped a good two feet, practically giving him whiplash. She turned on the blinding interrogation lamp as the words "last chance" flashed through his mind.

"Open up," she said.

He braced himself and waited for the games

to begin.

First came the captain's hook, scraping between his teeth and along his sensitive gum line. If this tool worked so well for the dentist, Seamus wondered if he could use it to catch fish—two, three, four at a time. The only more effective method would be dynamite. Then again, he disliked his dinner seasoned with nitroglycerin.

"Oh my," Grizelda said.

Seamus' eyes widened. "What?"

"How often do you floss?"

She moved the hook farther down his throat. His response escaped as a string of vowels, making "twice a day" sound like "ike a ay."

"Hmph."

Of course she doesn't believe me, Seamus thought. *She and her cigarette breath must know more about maintaining a healthy smile.*

"Turn your head to left," she said. "No. Too far. Back a little. Too far. Okay, don't move. Don't move."

With that, Grizelda dug her pickax into his gums, attempting to exhume an imaginary piece of popcorn or Jujube or treasure chest. The X that marked the spot she must've been focusing on was just the scar from his last visit.

He protested with a moan, which had little effect. In fact, Grizelda dug deeper. When she tried to remove her mechanical grip, the stainless steel hooked Seamus' tongue like a wide-mouth bass. His taster flapped as if splashing out of water, playing tug-of-war with the fishing line. He arched his back, trying to break free, but each squirm only worsened his situation.

"Hold still," she said, at last tearing the dental handshake from its catch.

She set the weapon down. She sat back as if Seamus had inconvenienced her, as if an action of his own volition had stopped her from completing her work, as if patient after patient had been sabotaging her good will and charity and his dissatisfaction was the straw that broke the hygienist's back.

"Your gums are bleeding," she said.

"Et's naw ma gums, et's ma tong."

"Rinse, please."

He choked back tears as he leaned over and downed the paper cup of tap water. He spat into the sink and watched the red swirl down the drain.

He knew a pastrami sandwich would never taste the same again. He knew he'd have to subsist on ice cream until the wound had healed. He wanted a vanilla soft serve from Fosters Freeze right then.

Seamus peered over his shoulder at his persecutor, who loudly exhaled as she checked the clock on the wall. He wasn't a violent person, but at that moment, he knew he could justify strangling her. No, too many witnesses. There were the staff members and the other patients to consider.

Wait.

That's it.

The other patients!

He wanted to launch from his chair and run down the halls, warning the other patients to turn back to save their teeth, tongues, and co-pays. These hygienists were out for blood with devices intended for mining and medieval warfare.

He'd run down the stairs, out the building, and up the street, fishing vest and dental bib flapping in the wind, to the next dentist's office and the next dentist's office to spread the news. Droves would follow Seamus on his quest. In time, he'd become the leader of the Global Dental Revolution. He'd blow the whistle on the likes of Grizelda and her fascist regime that supported cruel and unusual escapades in the name of preventing gingivitis.

Masochists would keep the old system afloat, but only for so long. Sadists like Grizelda soon would be out of a job and forced to resort to fetish clubs in Amsterdam, where the unassuming cotton scrubs would be replaced by the appropriate attire of leather, chains, and spikes.

That's when Seamus would instill a new dental procedure—one done with pillows and fairy dust. If a hygienist accidentally hurt their patient at any time, they would apologize, sincerely, and amend their transgression with a tarter-control lollipop. People would leave happy and say, "Thank you, Seamus." Yes. They'd say this to his smiling picture on the wall in every dental office.

Bronze monuments would be erected to honor the hero Seamus and his Crusade for Better Dental Care. He'd tour universities and visit with heads of state as a touted problem-solving guru. Then, with his free time, he'd fish the streams, lakes, and oceans of the world. He'd mount marlins and sharks on the walls of his Victorian estate as trophies of his mastery as an outdoorsman. Libraries and medical schools would be named in his honor. Parents would name their children after Seamus—Seamus the Great. Yes! And when those children would grow up, they'd tell others of their birth-name blessing and those people would say, "Wooww."

Yes, he could change the world one mouth at a time. Yet, he couldn't budge from his recliner. The pain was too great to move faster than slow motion.

He set down the paper cup and leaned back again. Grizelda, still waiting to continue, instructed him to open up. He obliged in fear of what would happen if he refused.

Seamus' tongue retreated to the recesses of his mouth every time the cold instrument brushed against it. After a few more close encounters with the hook of death, the poking and prodding ceased. It was finally time to clean those pearly whites and reds.

"What flavor do you want?" she asked.

He thought for a moment.

"Do you have a lollipop flavor?"

"Your choices are spearmint and peppermint."

He sighed and made his selection. Grizelda gorged the brushing bristles in the paste tin and went back to work. Seamus tasted steel, copper, and peppermint. He hoped she'd be done soon and avoided eye contact until the Almighty had answered his prayers.

"You need to brush and floss more," Grizelda

said. "We'll see you in six months."

"Any chance you won't be here in six months?"

She didn't seem to hear him. Maybe it was for the best.

He limped to the door and stopped. He didn't want to, but from force of habit and his general air of kindness, he said, "Have a nice day."

She smiled. Her face took a moment to figure out how to do it, but she smiled. He didn't know she was capable of such a feat.

The receptionist scheduled his next appointment, then slid him the colorful reminder card. Next to the penned date stood a happy tooth holding an oversized toothbrush. Seamus smothered the arrogant bastard in his vest pocket.

He turned the door handle and left the office. Finally, he was free to go fishing.

By the time he reached his car, his tongue had swollen to the size of a trout. He couldn't help but think of the fish he intended to catch an hour's drive from here. He thought of them swimming, doing what they had to do to get from point A to point B. He thought of Grizelda. And the chair. And the hook. And he sighed. Instead of heading north, he started his truck, drove to Fosters Freeze, and ordered a vanilla soft serve.

STRANGERS

Jesse sat alone at her bistro table outside the French café on Sunset. Her oversized glasses blocked the glare of the sun as well as the circles under her eyes. Fingering the corners of the paycheck, she thought four zeros weren't enough for three days of work. No amount was. The crisp angles indented the pads of her digits one by one, and the emerald lettering mocked her expired belief that the land under the sign was the modern Oz.

It all smelled like sawdust.

She quickly twice-folded the check and buried it in her pants pocket next to the Greyhound ticket. She found it curious how these people could be involved so secretly, so intimately, yet cut ties the moment they got what they wanted. Strangers of the worst sort. Jesse crossed her arms for warmth from a sudden chill.

An older man across the patio, who'd been

guzzling one cup of coffee after the other, continuously motioned the waiter for a waterfall of refills. He'd periodically caught her gaze over the past ten minutes or so. His silver mustache crowned a beguiling smile that reminded her of her grandfather—at least what she remembered of him anyway. He even had the same thoughtful wrinkles etched across his forehead.

Realizing she'd been staring at him for some time, she returned to a chapter in her guidebook. The pages had become wrinkled and dog-eared since she'd bought the paperback. Reading the words again this time, the story carried a different weight. It surveyed the history of Los Angeles, of how the Spanish explorer Gaspar de Portolà consecrated the land *El Pueblo de Nuestra Señora la Reina de los Angeles*—The Town of Our Lady the Queen of the Angels. People have even reported seeing ghosts—

"Where are you headed?" a voice said.

Jesse looked up to see that it was the old man who had interrupted her concentration. She acted as if she hadn't seen him before he spoke.

"Excuse me?"

He gestured to the canvas backpacks slumped at her feet. One of them had a black and pink patch with the word "Diva" stitched across it.

"Oh." Jesse exhaled. "Somewhere else."

Nearby laughter caught her attention. At the curb, Jesse saw two expensively dressed teenage girls loading their shopping bags into the trunk of their BMW. Their blond hair flickered under the California sun. With the tall flowers rising from the center of the boulevard behind them, the scene only lacked the postcard scribble, "Wish you were here."

She turned back to the guidebook. It said people have reported seeing ghosts of Spaniards or Native Americans along the Cahuenga Pass, originally an Indian burial ground, now a congested freeway snaking through the heart of Hollywood.

"Sounds like a nice place to visit," the old man said. He quietly chuckled as he stirred his drink with a teaspoon.

"What?"

"'Somewhere else.' Sounds like a nice place."

"Oh. Sorry. I was just reading this thing, and I thought— Never mind."

"You don't like LA?"

She eyed him suspiciously.

"I'm just curious," he continued. "That's all."

"Well... I don't know you, so..."

"Fair enough," he said, raising his hands in mock surrender.

She glanced across the street, past the potted trees, at the restaurant with yellow awnings and white tablecloths. She tried to keep her eyes on the diners in black suits and off the old man wearing the tweed blazer sitting one table over.

"New York," she said.

He hurried to swallow his sip. "What was that?"

"I'm going to New York."

"New York? Do you know anyone there?"

"No."

"Ever been to New York?"

"No."

He considered her answer for a moment. "You should go someplace more relaxed," he said. "Maybe see some old friends?"

She let the question hang in the air for a few seconds. She wondered if he was trying to sell something, whether this chitchat was a buildup to a product she couldn't live without for only three easy payments.

"There's no one I want to see," she said.

She watched him tear the corner off a sugar packet. He dumped the white grains, stirred, and began guzzling another cup.

"Don't you think it's a little too hot for coffee?"

He merrily licked his lips as he reached for more sugar. "It's never too hot for coffee."

She glanced at the weathered suitcase with the frayed straps nestled under his table. An ivory-colored Panama hat with a black band and bow rested atop the luggage.

"What about you?" she asked.

He slurped another helping of the steaming liquid.

"Just passing through. Heading back to my daughter's. Great kid. Sort of looked like you when she was your age."

With the condensation from the bottom of her cup of iced tea, Jesse twisted linking water rings onto the mosaic tabletop.

"Are you—" she spun another ring— "close

with your daughter?"

The old man smiled.

"I'm looking forward to seeing her. It's been a while." He extended a hand. "I'm James, by the way."

She shook it. His warm palm felt like cotton-threaded paper.

"Jesse."

His shoulders bounced with laughter.

"Jesse and James. What are the odds? Two notorious characters blending into the Sunset Strip. You look like a movie star. You a movie star?"

She turned away, tensing up again.

"Oh, I didn't mean anything by that. You just have that look like you're made for pictures."

She managed a smile that folded into a sullen laugh. "My grandmother was one once. I used to dress up in these old costumes she had and put on plays for her and my grandfather in their living room."

"See. It's in the blood."

"I used to get in trouble for spending too much time there," she said. "But they both died when I was ten."

"Sorry to hear that."

She shrugged. Took a sip of her drink.

"You from here?" she asked.

"Oh, no. Lived here for many years. Came to get more sunshine. Saw this town when it used to be something. But now it's time for me to go back north, back to the Sound."

Her attention reinvigorated. "Puget Sound?"

"The one and only."

"That's where I'm from. Which part?"

"Kingston, across from Seattle."

"I'm from Tacoma."

"Well, I'll say. You know what I miss about Seattle? The coffee."

"You seem to be enjoying the coffee down here just fine."

"It'll do. For now. But do you know the main ingredient to a good cup of coffee? Water. Seattle has some *great* water. Not like that LA liquid with all the brown stuff swimming around in it, you know what I mean? I don't trust a glass of water if it looks back at me."

She leaned into her shoulder to hide her grin.

"That's why I can't wait to get back there," he said. "The water. And my daughter." His smile faded into a pensive expression. "God, I miss her. You know, Jesse, to be honest, I wasn't the best dad to her growing up. I uh...I just wish I was around more, you know?"

She watched him intently as he bit down on his lips. The passing waiter anticipated James' next request and refilled his porcelain cup, accidentally spilling a few drops onto the saucer underneath.

"Thank you very much." He tore open another sugar packet. "Your family didn't come down with you?"

His question sounded more like a statement.

"No," she said.

"You miss them?"

She looked toward the street.

"No."

"Well, that's not a nice sentiment to have."

"You don't know them."

He waited for her to elaborate as if he had all the time in the world. She looked him over once more and exhaled.

"I do miss my brother," she admitted.

"You two close?"

"Were."

"He used to look after you, huh?"

Her stomach turned. Her skin flushed and tingled as she sat up and squared off with the old man. "How do you know that's what happened? Have you been following me or something?"

She didn't want to tell him anything more. She wanted to grab her drink and vanish. Hit the road. She'd done it before. Yet her feet felt as heavy as anvils, and the old man's tranquil gaze had already begun to calm her breathing despite her will.

"No," he said, "I haven't been following you. It's your face. It tells me everything."

She settled back in her chair and crossed her arms.

Two stores down, she saw a group of Japanese tourists hungrily snapping photographs of the Sunset Boulevard sign. Then they turned their cameras to the marble facades of the restaurants, nightclubs, and specialty stores. She wanted to tell them to go home; the streets weren't paved with gold. If they really wanted to make their trip worthwhile, they should try to find all those Spanish ghosts.

She tried not to look at James again. That's when his voice deepened, sounding even more like her grandfather. He asked, "When was the last time you talked to your brother?"

She sucked the rest of her iced tea through the straw until it slurped, until there was nothing left to justify her hesitation.

"Before I left," she said. "I told him I could take care of myself."

"So you came down here to be a star, huh? To make it on your own?" His gaze grew more deliberate. "To find out who you are?"

"I did meet a producer a few weeks ago. Said he was going to give me my big chance."

"I've heard that before."

"Me, too. I just never thought it would happen to me."

She ran her fingertips over her guidebook, now resting shut on the table.

James was about to take another sip of coffee but set down his cup instead.

"You know what I also miss about Seattle? There's this pizzeria up on Broadway. Pagliacci. I used to take my daughter there all the time. Great garlic bread."

She knew it well. Her brother used to take her there on Fridays after school. He'd let her order whatever she wanted. Then they'd fill up on ice cream at Henry's Parlor down the street. She remembered how her hand would disappear into his massive mitt as they walked back to their apartment, kicking up leaves as they went. He made her feel safe. Feel at home.

There weren't any leaves on Sunset. She bowed her head as a tear slid down the side of her nose.

James threw his head back to fling the last drop of coffee into his mouth. He smacked his lips and released a pleasured sigh.

"Well, must be going. Have a flight to catch. Good luck with your acting, if you decide to pursue it. It was nice talking with you. Maybe I'll run into you someday up north."

She gently nodded.

He flipped the Panama hat onto his head and adjusted the brim. He left a generous tip and began walking out of the patio when he stopped at the waist-high gate. James pulled a white handkerchief from his blazer pocket, set it across the cover of Jesse's guidebook.

"You know," he said, "we all get lost sometimes. When we're found again...that's the greatest joy."

He tipped his hat and meandered down the street with a relaxed gait that seemed ethereal. Halfway down the block he nodded at a preoccupied mother pushing a stroller on her afternoon workout. A serene expression washed over her face as she returned the smile and continued forward with an extra bounce in her step.

Jesse wondered why he had stayed in this town for so long, what he'd found after so many years. A few passersby cast shadows over her as they crossed the sun. She watched their silhouettes float over the ground and thought of ghosts again. She wondered if people were drawn to this city because phantoms or spirits, or whatever you wanted to call them, existed in a place supposedly protected by angels. Maybe they just wanted to check out the dichotomy for themselves.

She reached into her pocket, her fingers finding the Greyhound ticket. She pulled it out, rubbed her thumbs over the text, then wondered if it was raining in Tacoma.

She found it strange that, in a city of over three million people, James was the only person who actually saw her. Not wanting to let go just yet, she turned around to catch a final glimpse of him, but he had already disappeared into the sunlight.

KILLING BIRDS

Tommy ran into the house, and the backyard was quiet again. The gun felt cold in my hand. I dropped it on the ground and just stood there, awaiting a cue of some sort that never arrived.

I walked to the corner where the bird had fallen. One eye laid open, frozen with the same troubled face it had after the first shot passed straight through. I could see the BB-sized wound in its chest. And the one in its neck. No blood flowed from either.

My hands dug a hole in a shady spot. I gently picked up the bird, rested it in my makeshift grave, and covered its feathers with the chilled soil.

I didn't wait for Tommy to return. I didn't even want to see him. I hid the gun behind the stack of apple boxes where spiders had strewn webs between the wall and the wood. I shook the silken threads from my dirt-streaked fingers and jumped over the cinderblock wall into the alley between the houses. I couldn't leave through the front.

And all the way home I hid from passing cars. I didn't want to be seen, or caught, for I didn't know what would happen to me, or who knew. I thought of the bird right after I'd shot it. I thought of how it remained perched on the wire despite the pain it must have felt. I remembered now that it looked proud—and beautiful. And I wondered why we did such things to birds.

TODAY'S THE DAY

Today, H tells himself. Today's the day.

Crouched over, he presses his left arm to his stomach for warmth, for comfort. Waiting on the steel examination table, he rolls his fingers to keep his limb from going stiff. After too much stretching he flinches, lets his arm dangle.

Even the table's cold. It rocks from corner to corner with every minor move.

He considers his surroundings and shakes his head. He can't believe he's here. But today, he's decided, is the day he tells the entering doctor.

"So how's everything been—" the doctor glances at his chart— "H?"

"Not bad."

The physician proceeds with his customary examination. He shines a light in his patient's eyes, checks his throat, takes his pulse. The doctor lifts the patient's wrist, but H cringes and pulls away.

"Something wrong?"

"I hurt my arm. Playing baseball the other day. Threw it out."

"Well, you just rest it then. Anything else?"

"Actually, doc. I have this..." He trails off.

"Yes?"

But today's the day.

"Never mind."

H exits the front door of the clinic. He hobbles down Third, hangs a right at Park, and heads home. Today was the day.

He climbs the drafty, cement stairwell of his apartment building. Sticks his crooked key in the lock. Today was the day.

He enters the tenement. Stark possessions and papers are scattered in no particular fashion. It looks as though someone has torn the place apart trying to find their fix. Ignoring the mess, H lights a candle on the coffee table. The spoon sizzles. He rolls up his sleeve. Veins budge in blacks and reds. Bruised tissue collapses. Track marks like staples violently removed. H ties off. He pushes off.

Tomorrow.

Tomorrow is the day.

THE LOOKOUT

An eerie calm settles in as you buckle yourself into the driver's seat. The Mustang's engine bellows to life, and you smile for the first time in months. Four months and thirteen days, to be precise.

In the passenger seat, Ashley gives you a nod, so you pull out of the driveway as the sky turns from navy blue to black. Then again, it's never truly black in LA—more like a charcoal haze dusted with the orange glow of streetlamps. It's always darker by your house since the canyon ridges block the sun, but you'll get a second chance at the light once you leave again.

Away from the hills, the evening sky looks like a palette of pastels. This is exactly what you need. You're going to enjoy tonight because, every time you start to drive, you fear the two of you won't have another like it. You just need a place to relax, a place to be together.

The lookout.

That's where you'll go.

You drive west down Ventura Boulevard, a lively stretch of bars, clothing shops, and restaurants. A silver Charger and red Camaro race down the opposite lane. Several months ago you would have taken part in the fun.

Ashley points to the '50s-themed Mel's Diner where some local band and their friends monopolize the front corner. They sit and stand in contorted positions and, as a whole, look like an all-American Picasso painting. One guy with excessively tall spiked hair, a style only rock stars can get away with, sits atop the cream leather booth strumming his guitar while girls adorn the bench around him. They gaze up with spangled eyes, and everyone animatedly sings along. This must be a common occurrence since they have synchronized hand gestures.

"That's where we had our first date," Ashley says.

"How could I forget?" You watch her brush an auburn curl behind her ear. "Except I'm taking you someplace even better."

She doesn't say anything, but gives you a knowing look. You love her dimples when she smiles.

Without warning, your left hand begins to shake. Nerves again. Ashley's grin changes to a frown of concern. You quickly stretch your fingers as if it's nothing and focus out the window.

Traffic stops you in front of an old movie palace. Its heyday is long gone, and the neon marquee tells of its conversion into a Barnes and Noble. Customers browse the shelves erected behind the Art Deco facade of the forgotten theatre, while others form a line down the block for a book signing. The author greets each enthusiast with a smile and a stroke of her pen.

People used to be happy to see you like that. Now your family and friends only have condolences since the accident. A person can only hear "I'm so sorry" a limited number of times. So you escape in your car, despite their concerns that you're behind the wheel so often, let alone at all. They wouldn't understand the reason for your wanderlust anyway.

As if Ashley knows what you're thinking, she says, "At least we can drive together."

You pass three or four Starbucks coffee houses. After a while it's difficult to keep track of how many you come across in this town. Outside the last one, a brunette with mysterious slits for eyes sits on her boyfriend's lap. He wraps her in his coat to shield her from an unusually cold breeze. They take turns sipping a coffee. Their mouths breathe the steam of passion, the steam of candied caffeine, which is reinvigorated when their lips come together for a prolonged kiss.

That's the way Ashley used to kiss you. Seeing her buckled into the next seat only accentuates the void between you now, for her lips aren't on yours anymore. Your hands can no longer drive up her back, sliding her skin between the canals of your fingers anymore. After long days at work, you can't come home, curl up on the couch, and listen to each other…breathing…until you both fall asleep. Just yesterday, and every day since the crash, getting any substantial rest has been nearly impossible.

The two of you were on the way to the lookout when it happened. Ashley saw the deer just as it ran down the hillside and into the road. You swerved to avoid the doe but lost control when the tires hit that patch of gravel. The police said you were not at fault. The doctors told you there was nothing more you could do; the impact was too sudden. "Your wife didn't suffer," they said. Their words wrapped around your lungs like fingers and squeezed.

Now your only peace is the lookout.

To get to there, you drive between the mountains up the sinuous 405 freeway toward Mulholland. You roll down the windows and feel the June air flow over your head, around your ears, and down your neck like warm gobs of honey. You feel it more distinctly than ever before.

You exit at the top of the Santa Monica Mountains and drive west. The canyon walls on either side cast shadows over the dashboard. Up here, the car guides you onto familiar streets until the houses pull back into the trees.

The Mustang continues past the accident site, where you can still see yourself holding her, until you reach the small embankment most people could easily miss. Dirt grinds under the tires as you pull off to the side of the road and shift into park. You've come here countless times to get away from the city, away from the hassles of the job, away from yourself. You remember the times you brought Ashley, how it became your special place, eventually the place you proposed. You can almost smell her honeysuckle perfume.

"Thanks for bringing me here," she says.

Her voice fills you with that familiar warmth.

"Thanks for being here," you say.

She tucks her face against her shoulder to hide the humble smile she gets when you flatter her, the expression you'd give endless compliments to see as often as possible. You reach over and run your hand up her nape and into her large, auburn curls—the way she likes it. Then you smell your fingertips—the way you like it.

She laces her fingers between yours, and you never want to stop her from looking at you.

This time, you won't let her go.

You give your wedding band a single turn, then put the car in gear. As the sun finally begins to set, the pink and purple rays illuminate your fall down the mountain, back into the valley, where the streetlights and house lights and store lights shine in all directions like a constellation of stars. They welcome you into the new nightfall as you embrace the thrill of weightlessness—reaching, with outstretched fingers to grasp the cherry beams of sunlight.

ACKNOWLEDGEMENTS

FIRST THINGS FIRST: I wish to thank you, reader, for picking up a copy of my debut collection of short stories. This chapbook marks my foray into the world of independent publishing that is taking the literary world by storm, and I'm excited to have you along for the ride.

When my fiancée and I first got together and she learned I was a published author, I handed her the anthology containing "Killing Birds" and "Today's the Day." As you've now seen, the tales are a tad dark. She looked up after finishing them with a worried look in her eye and said, "But you seem like such a happy person."

I am. Honestly. I'm even happier now that I'm able to bundle these previously published and world premiere stories together under one title.

A special thanks goes to my readers Meghan Zuck, Eduardo Mendoza, and Kelly McDonald, whose insights only improved the tales you've just read. I'm also indebted to Shelley Berman, Shelly Lowenkopf, Patty Seyburn, Aram Saroyan, and TC Boyle, who gave valuable feedback through the various incarnations of these stories. Thanks to my peers at the USC Professional Writing Program, especially fellow author and friend Will Entrekin for his input and encouragement on my first e-book endeavor. Finally, I am grateful to my family and friends who supported my writing through the years. You never made me feel crazy for doing what I love.

ABOUT THE AUTHOR

DANIEL GARDINA is a writer living in Los Angeles. He earned his BA and MFA from the University of Southern California, where he studied with authors such as John Rechy, Aram Saroyan, Gregg Hurwitz, and TC Boyle. He wrote his first novel, *The Last Night*, two different times—the second attempt was much better—and he's currently working on the next book. In the meantime, he writes the *Hollywood Novelist* blog at www.danielgardina.com.

AN EXCERPT FROM THE NOVEL
The Last Night

Pine and eucalyptus trees surrounded the Westfield Academy baseball diamond, forging a sort of haven where the only sight was dusk overhead. I felt I was somewhere far away in the mountains, in another world entirely, forgetting that just past the trees and through the winding passageways of Coldwater Canyon lay metropolitan LA.

This was a welcomed escape.

When I stepped onto the field for the first time in almost nine years, with that sharp smell of freshly cut grass still warm from the summer sun, I couldn't help but think of all the nights I'd spent here before I left for college. I felt the familiar grind of infield dirt beneath my shoes. My head hung low to watch my feet balance along the first base line, to see my toe drag across the chalk as it created a white crescent against the earth. I saw myself back when I used to play, fielding grounders at shortstop and throwing the ball to Alex at first. Those were our simple times.

Some part of me still was that person, but the rest knew I could never be the same again. If only I could reach out and touch my former self. I didn't know what I'd hoped to get back. Maybe I just didn't want to know what I do now.

I thought of all the players who rounded the bases on this very soil fifty years ago; how nothing else could have mattered than the crack of the bat, their teammates' cheers from the dugout, the smell of dirt woven in the seams of leather gloves. I could almost see those ballplayers, feel them, before they faded into the evening light, never to return except in memory.

No one knew I was here, especially not Shannon. What would she care anyway? I could have been driving off the edge of the Santa Monica Mountains and she wouldn't know the difference.

No.

I kicked the dirt at the idea. I kicked it again at the thought of her walking away. I'd taken the long road to return to where I'd begun when it was just me, whoever that was, when no one else told me who I was supposed to become. I'd returned to the place where I'd met her. Where I'd met Alex.

My phone rang, and my heart jumped when I hoped that it was him, that somehow he knew I was thinking of him just then. It wasn't. Then my chest started to burn. What the hell was I doing here? I'd disappeared when he needed me most. Alex had saved my life, and I might have failed to repay the favor.

ONE WEEK EARLIER

CHAPTER ONE

My black Mustang GT sped through traffic, as fast as one can in rush hour anyway, to arrive at Shannon's first recital since earning her master's degree. I snuck in after the show had begun and found a seat in the back just in time. She took center stage in the Ralph Lauren dress I bought her for our last anniversary. She flipped her auburn curls over her shoulder, then readied the violin under her chin. She stood perfectly poised, almost statuesque, until the hairs of her bow glided over the instrument's strings and Beethoven's "Violin Romance" radiated over the audience.

I couldn't think of how many times I'd heard the composition. During the weeks of honing her performance, I'd turn down the volume of the Dodger game on TV, hold still to quiet the groans of the leather armchair, and watch the home team run the bases to the music seeping through the closed bedroom door. Now, from the back of the recital hall, I could see the patrons were as enraptured as I had been. I may be biased, but she was the best violinist I'd ever heard. Tonight was the first time I'd listened to the song with accompaniment. The orchestra made her sound even better.

After the show, I gave her a kiss to congratulate her, but her attention was focused on the surrounding people in suits and black-framed glasses. They must have been important because, each time I tried to get her attention, she'd wave at me as if to say, *One more minute, Ed.*

One minute turned into thirty, then fifty, and then I lost count. At first glance, my suit was just as nice as these people's. Yet I didn't belong. The other musicians and guests who didn't acknowledge my presence only reinforced that fact. My musical talent was limited to the guitar lessons my father gave me ages ago. I just didn't have the patience for the snobbery that often accompanied the music business. Somehow Shannon could tolerate the games, even if she didn't play into them herself. I signaled toward the door to let her know I'd meet her at home, but I doubt she saw me.

My post-graduate life was spent in a cubicle punching keys as resident code monkey for LA's leading consulting firm. When people asked how I enjoyed my job in IT, I said, "It pays the bills." I'd spent the last year developing a database for a start-up Internet marketplace aimed at shrinking Amazon's piece of the pie. I was convinced the client would later file for bankruptcy when it failed to compete, which would negate all the long nights I'd sacrificed. I regularly reminded myself that the paycheck afforded my coveted, Westside apartment with the creakiest door in the building.

I tossed my keys on the foyer table and strolled toward the far wall of windows. I surveyed the darkened basin below. The city lights were laid out like stars under the charcoal haze of a sky. I exhaled, weaving my fingers behind my head, relishing my slice of the twentysomething American Dream.

Shannon returned home near midnight. She walked in sporting jeans and her black blazer, the Ralph Lauren draped over her arm in a garment bag. I played solitaire on the kitchen countertop. She strode past me to lay her dress and violin on the couch as I flipped over three more cards, none of which I needed.

"I really enjoyed that."

She spun around as her hand shot to her chest.

"You scared me," she said. "I thought you'd be asleep."

I uncovered the ace of spades and moved it up top to start a new foundation. She slid into the barstool next to mine.

"I fumbled the bridge a little," she said.

"Didn't even notice."

She tried not to grin. "Liar." She moved the two of spades onto the ace. I didn't know how she saw that simple move and I missed it. She continued, "Why did you leave so quickly?"

"You were busy talking. I didn't want to interrupt."

"Do you know who those people were?"

I shook my head, keeping my eyes on the cards.

"Friends of my advisor," she said. "One was from the LA Phil, another from Baltimore. The Baltimore woman remembered my audition from last month."

"Why don't you sound excited?"

"Because I'm wondering why you aren't."

I stopped flipping cards and collected them back into the box. "I'm just tired. Too tired to even finish this game. Really, I'm proud of you." I kissed her forehead and returned the deck to the coffee table drawer.

"This could mean big things for us," she said. "Have you thought about my question?"

I studied the city lights through the windows. There were fewer than earlier. I hoped that if I concentrated hard enough they'd spell out an answer for me. Aside from a line of blinking red bulbs atop a skyscraper, the rest remained still.

"It's just not part of my plan right now," I said. "I want to be sure I have a good job before I start a family."

"I'm not talking children here." She stood to join me, lacing her fingers between mine. "I'm talking us."

We'd been though this discussion a few times. I didn't hate the topic. I hated the uncertainty of having broken up before and what that meant for the future. For *us*.

Back in college, the last time we were apart, I'd shown up at one of her recitals, very much like tonight. She exited the performance wearing that black blazer, again with one hand carrying her violin case while the other held a garment bag. When she saw me, some brand of sad pleasure crossed her face—at least I'd hoped it was pleasure. She decided to approach anyway. Her auburn curls bounced over her apple cheeks and gently tapped her shoulders. They were the same curls I used to run my hands through—the way she liked it—before I'd smell my fingertips, allowing traces of her honeysuckle conditioner to wander into my nostrils—the way I liked it. The moment was as intimate as it was foreign because it had been banished to memory.

As we walked to her car she said, "I saw you after the show, you know. Standing in the back."

"I said I would come."

"That was before..."

She stopped herself. Before she could begin again, I jumped right in and said, "I want to give us another shot."

I'd never spoken so plainly before. I liked it. I could see her attempting to sort the unsolicited information, but she didn't smile as I'd hoped.

"Ed. I'm seeing someone."

"That Richie guy?"

She gave me a stern look for being cute with her. "His name's Rich. He's nice."

"He sounds wonderful. Does he love you?"

She tried to balance the dress and violin while fumbling through her purse. "It's too soon. We've only been seeing each other for a month."

"Perfect," I said. "Best to let him go before he gets too attached."

"You can't come here and tell me you want to get back together."

"You just left. I don't know what to do with that."

She sighed. "It wasn't all your fault. I could have been more communicative, too."

I slowed to delay reaching her car since each step was another grain down the hourglass. My effort was useless, though. Her Toyota was now two spaces away and the keys rattled in her hand.

"So let's talk," I said. "If you're hesitating for even a moment, let's figure this out."

Now she huffed and looked away. "I can't do this tonight."

That much was true. The next morning was something different all together. After I flipped on the news and threw a slice of wheat bread in the toaster oven, I heard the front door shake. Someone tried the knob, but finding it locked, they rang the bell. I figured my roommate had forgotten his key again.

When I opened the door, however, Shannon turned to face me, her hair whipping across her face.

I stopped breathing. She breathed heavily, not daring to blink her hazel eyes. I took half a step toward her. She came the rest of the way and wrapped her arms around me. After a moment, I pulled her to my chest.

Her hair smelled of honeysuckle.

Back in the kitchen, she sat at the counter while I fried eggs and potatoes. We ate with the TV volume turned down and with her knee pressed against mine the entire meal.

That was then. Now in the apartment we shared, she was the one asking me to come back, and I couldn't fathom what was keeping me away. Knowing what I'd done to save *us* before, the role reversal knotted my stomach.

"I don't know what's stopping me," I said, squeezing her fingers in kind. "But it's something. I can't ignore that."

She dropped my hands and treaded toward the bedroom. She took off her blazer, stopped, and pointed the jacket at me like a weapon. "You need to get out of your head. You paralyze yourself."

"Are you saying I should ignore reason and just say yes?"

My laptop chimed at the head of the dining table: a new e-mail received. I instinctively moved to read it, reacting to the bell like one of Pavlov's dogs. Shannon's face flushed, so I halted mid-step. We squared off on opposite ends of the wooden slab.

"All I'm saying is that every choice can't perfectly match your list of bullet points. I need to know if you *want* to marry me."

The computer chimed again. I knew she hated that sound after hours.

"I'm not going to beg you, Ed. You either do or you don't. I just don't know how much longer I'm going to wait."

She stormed into the bedroom. I wanted to run after her but had no idea what I would say when I got there. Instead, I resigned to silence the computer. I didn't care who sent the message and closed the program. That's when an unexpected name caught my eye.

I reopened the mailbox. One new message, which simply read:

> last weekend of my exhibit. hope you can make it. ashley left.   — alex

Since his wedding three years ago, I hadn't heard much more from Alex Evergreen than the fliers advertising his artwork and a couple Christmas cards. The most recent included a picture of he and Ashley hugging in front of their recently purchased California Craftsman, the words "Seasons Greetings" scripted in red across the upper corner.

I reviewed the last two words to make certain I hadn't misread them. "Ashley left." They were clear; yet they didn't make sense. He had friends to lean on up north. Brian and Meghan were part of his new family now. Still, I would have expected at least a phone call if his marriage was on the verge of collapse.

I dialed him right away. His contact held the

first slot in my phone book. I saw it often, but clicking on his name created an unfamiliar aftertaste. I waited through the longest three rings before a quiet "hello" trickled through the line.

"Alex? It's Ed. I just got your e-mail. What happened?"

He sounded like a diseased man trying to choke out his final words. "Can you come?"

I stood up. I'd always been unable to sit still during important conversations, but I fought my usual desire to pace in circles over the carpet.

"Talk to me," I said. "Tell me what's going on."

More rasping breaths.

"Can you come?"

I headed directly to the bedroom closet and plucked shirts from the hangers. Shannon, already dressed in her penguin pajamas, stepped out from the bathroom as I pulled a duffle from under the bed. She tried to say something but couldn't. Then it dawned on me how this looked.

"No," I said, "I'm not leaving you. But I have to fly to Seattle in the morning."

"Can't someone else at the office go?"

"The office isn't sending me anywhere."

She couldn't fathom what was going on. I told her about the e-mail and the phone call. Her guard dropped. I watched as her expression battled between frustration with me and concern for Alex's predicament. She stopped to compose herself.

"So you go at the drop of a hat for Alex after… what…a three-year absence, but you won't…"

I was glad she decided not to finish her thought.

Before I had a chance to think, I said, "Maybe this time away from each other will be good for us." I immediately regretted it.

A look sparked in her eye. I knew it well. She was about to fire off an ironclad rebuttal I wasn't going to like. Finally, she said: "This isn't a problem for Brian and Meghan."

"Please don't compare us to them." I threw rolled pairs of socks into the duffle. "They're the high school sweethearts everyone fawns over at ten-year reunions."

"And we can't have that?"

I laid the bag on the floor and walked to her, scooping her hands into mine. I couldn't tell whether her eyes screamed that she loved me or wanted to kill me. Probably both.

I said, "Alex and Ashley split up after only three years of marriage. I want to be sure about us."

After enough time passed for those words to sink in, her hands finally touched back.

"You're not seriously going tomorrow, are you?"

"I have to."

I thumbed the top of her lotioned hands.

"I owe him."

She swallowed her displeasure in the way I'd come to admire. I never doubted how much she loved me. I just hoped she didn't doubt the same. I pulled a hair stuck to her lips and moved it behind her ear. Her smile was effortless. Comfortable. Home.

Then her slight pleasure hardened.

"You may owe him," she said. "But you're sleeping on the couch tonight."